BLUE & BERTIE

To Mum and Dad
KL

SIMON AND SCHUSTER
First published in Great Britain in 2016 by Simon and Schuster UK Ltd
1st Floor, 222 Gray's Inn Road, London WC1X 8HB
A CBS Company
Text and illustrations copyright © 2016 Kristyna Litten
The right of Kristyna Litten to be identified as the author and illustrator of this work has been
asserted by her in accordance with the Copyright, Designs and Patents Act, 1988

A CIP catalogue record for this book is available from the British Library upon request
ISBN: 978-1-4711-2373-3 (HB)
ISBN: 978-1-4711-2374-0 (PB)
ISBN: 978-1-4711-2375-7 (eBook)
Printed in China
2 4 6 8 10 9 7 5 3 1

KRISTYNA LITTEN

BLUE & BERTIE

SIMON AND SCHUSTER
London   New York   Sydney   Toronto   New Delhi

EVERY DAY *Bertie and the giraffes did the* **same thing** *at the* **same time.** **Crunchity-crunch** *– they nibbled sweet leaves from the tops of the trees.*

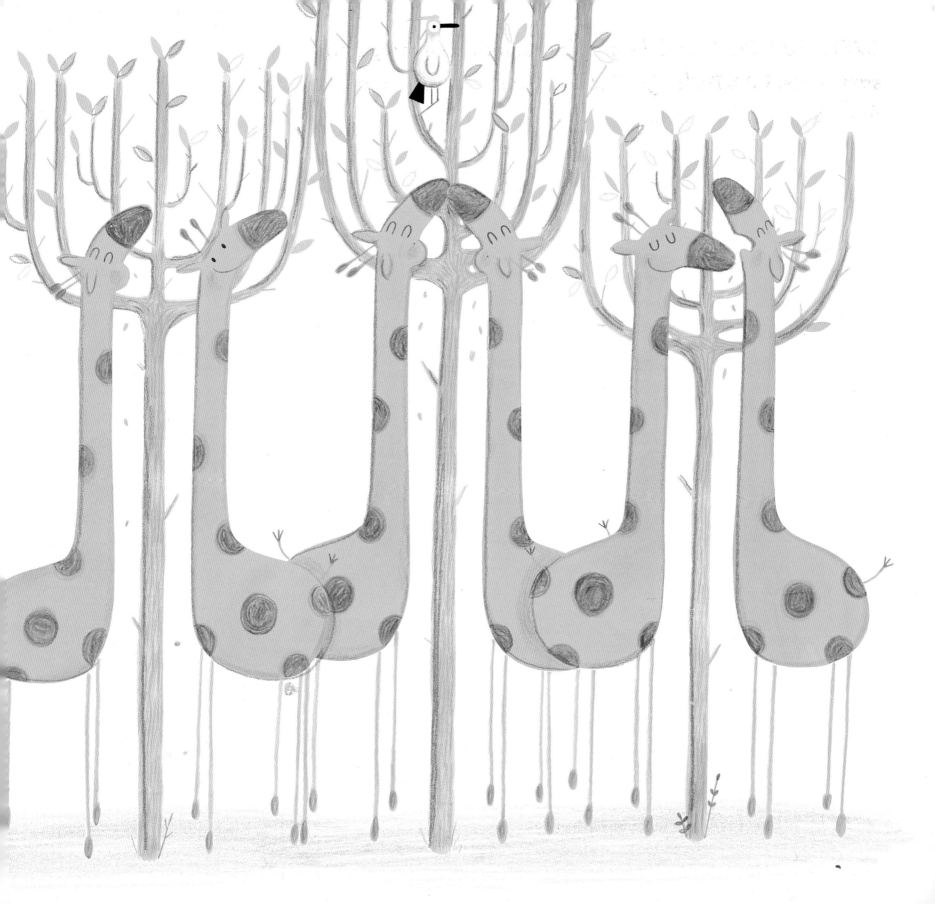

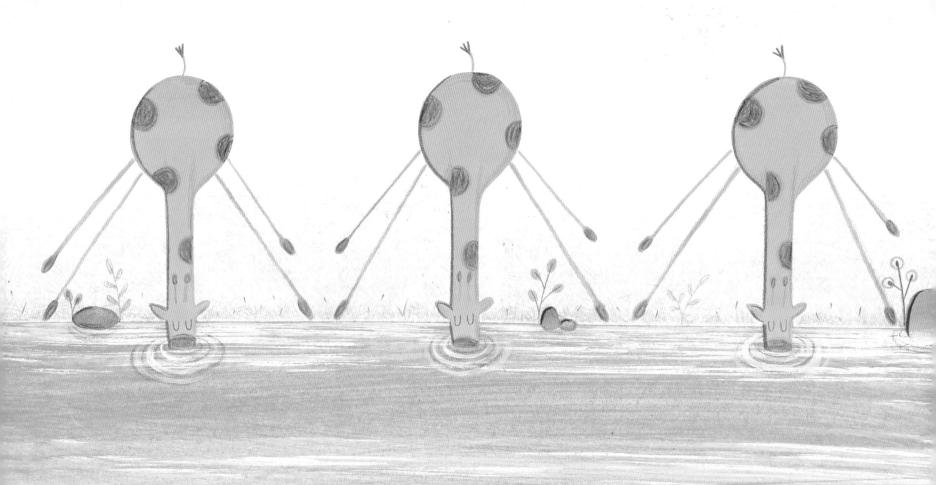

Sip, slurp – *they took a cooling drink at the watering-hole.*

And when they were tired, they
curled their long necks, and
snore, snore, snore
– they snoozed.

EACH DAY was much like the last
and that was JUST HOW THEY LIKED IT.

Crunchity-crunch
Sip, slurp
Snore, snore, snore.

And then, ONE DAY. . .

BERTIE OVERSLEPT!

*When he woke up, he realised he was **alone**,*
and HE'D NEVER BEEN ON HIS OWN BEFORE.

'*What shall I do?*
What shall I do?' *said Bertie.*

'*Should I go left?* **Or right?**

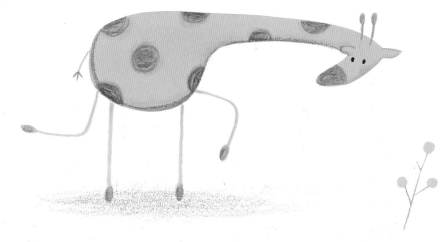

Straight ahead? **Or back?**'

BERTIE WAS LOST.

Soon large salty tears were sliding down his cheeks.
HOW WAS HE GOING TO GET HOME?

SUDDENLY, *Bertie heard a noise.*

'Hello?' he said. 'Who's there?'

'I can see you,' said Bertie, bravely. 'And I'm **not** afraid.'

'I might be a little bit afraid of you, though,' said the creature, stepping forward shyly.

BERTIE WAS AMAZED.
The creature was just like him, only he was – **BLUE.**

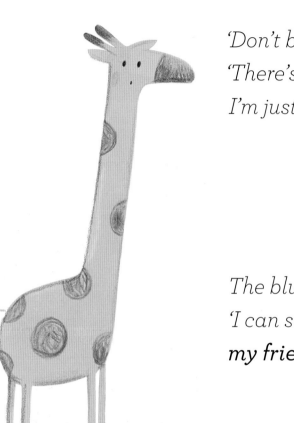

'*Don't be silly,*' *said Bertie at last.*
'*There's nothing to be afraid of.*
I'm just a lost giraffe.'

The blue giraffe smiled.
'*I can show you the way home,*
my friend,' *he said.* '*If you like.*'

BERTIE DID LIKE.

So **trit trot, trit trot,** off they went together.

'You all right there, **my friend**?' asked Blue.

'Very all right,' said Bertie. 'I never knew all this was here!'

Trit trot, trit trot,
on they went together.

'Wow!' said Bertie.
'Look at all this!'

'These are the rarest flowers in the world,' said Blue, smiling.

Then . . .

Gallopy-gallopy-gallopy – WHOOSH!

'I feel free!' cried Bertie.

*'You are free, **my friend**, you are,'* said Blue.

It was a wonderful journey.
'I never knew there was so much to see,'
breathed Bertie. 'Thank you, Blue.'

'Why don't we do it again, tomorrow?'
said Blue.
'I can't,' said Bertie. 'I have to **crunch,
sip** and **snore** with all the others.'

'Oh,' said Blue, sadly.
'Well, in that case . . .

...*your herd is just over there.'*

'So it is!' said Bertie.
'Hello! Hello! It's me,
I'm home everybody!'

'Bye, Bertie,' said Blue, and he turned to leave.

'Blue, wait!' called Bertie. 'Aren't you coming?'

Blue hesitated.

'But I'm different,' he said.

'Trust me, **my friend,**' said Bertie.

Bertie was right.
Blue fitted in **perfectly!**

FROM THEN ON, *the herd still* **crunched** *and* **sipped** *and* **snoozed.** *But now they did things a little bit differently each day.*

AND THAT WAS JUST HOW THEY LIKED IT.

BEST OF ALL, *Blue and Bertie*
remained **the very best of friends.**